I0684168

DARSIMEON GONE

KIERAN WIESENBERG

Darsimeon Gone is a work of fiction. Names, characters, places, and incidents are either the product of the author's imagination or are used fictitiously. Any resemblance to actual events, locales, or persons, living or dead, is entirely coincidental.

Copyright © 2025 by Kieran Wiesenberg

All rights reserved.

No portion of this book may be reproduced in any form without written permission from the publisher or author, except as permitted by U.S. copyright law.

For rights inquiries, permissions, or additional information, please contact:

info@kieranwiesenberg.com

www.kieranwiesenberg.com

Darsimeon Gone / Kieran Wiesenberg. — First edition

ISBN 979-8-9860007-4-9

Cover illustration and design by Kieran Wiesenberg

CONTENTS

For Gram

THE SEVEN GENRES

There are seven genres of magic in this world. Seven forms by which arcana can be reliably manipulated by the arcane. They are as follows.

Burn - The magic of fire, heat, and flame

Drip - The magic of water, vapor, and ice

Quake - The magic of earth, rock, and root

Gust - The magic of wind, air, and storms

Shade - The magic of darkness, shadow, and gloom

Glow - The magic of light, color, and life

Bleed - The magic of blood, bone, and decay

DARSIMEON GONE

I t all started when Professor Ludregard's cat went missing. Naturally, everyone was a suspect.

"I expect to have this sorted by the end of the day," she said, addressing us from the front of the brightly lit classroom. "Should no explanation present itself by then, I fear I'll have no choice but to hold everyone accountable."

The professor gazed down then, looked to the cushion on her desk where Darsimeon always sat—now an empty, cat-shaped crevasse—and looked up again. Her eyes, normally bright and twinkling, now wavered with tears.

"Very well," she said quickly, turning before any could run. She then fled the class, and the minute she did, all the lights in the room dimmed slightly. It seemed that even in her darkest of moods, the professor could not help but exude light.

I was determined to make it so again.

"Right then," I said, standing up and striding to the front of the room. It was not a large class, Introduction to Glow. Only nine of us in all. Not large, though sufficient enough to make narrowing down a guilty party somewhat tricky. Tricky, but not impossible.

"Who was it?" I asked simply, taking the time to narrow my eyes at each and every classmate. "Speak now and save us all the time of eking you out. Or worse, taking your blame."

When no one spoke after a moment, my eyes narrowed further.

"Well?" I said. "I *know* it was one of you."

"Now hold on a minute, Izra," said Bronte, a tall, brown canine sat near the front. "What makes you so sure?"

"The same thing that assures Professor Ludregard," I explained. *"Opportunity."*

"Opportunity?" echoed Suzetta, a round-faced girl whose nose seemed to be perpetually buried in a handkerchief.

"Precisely," I said, and in a fluid motion raised an article that had been sitting on the professor's desk. It was the classroom's after hours entry log.

"According to this, a number of persons entered this classroom last night. The same number of persons who are currently in this room.

"Bronte, Bravel, Suzetta, Guyland, Rula, and Torrin," I said, listing off the names in sequence. "Each of you were here at some point in the night. Meaning each of you had the opportunity to abscond with the professor's beloved cat. And, given Darsimeon's—er...shall we say, *less than agile* nature, I'd say all of you had the *means* as well. That, of course, leaves *motive*, something I believe will reveal itself with but a little prodding."

"Prodding, eh?" said Bravel, an irritable boy in every sense, to the class. "What d'you reckon she means by that?"

"I mean, Bravel, that I'm going to ask you questions. You're going to answer my questions, and in answering them—whether you'd like to or not—you're going to tell me exactly what happened here. Why Darsimeon has gone from us, and who of you is responsible."

"Who of *us*?" someone echoed, and there was a grumbling of mutual dissent.

"That's what I said, yes."

"To be fair, Izra," came Bronte, ever diplomatic, "what makes you so sure it was one of us? How do we know the cat didn't just—I don't know...*wander off?*

I sighed. "Bronte, in all your time here at Avenwood, have you ever once seen Darsimeon leave this classroom?"

The large canine considered. "Erm...no."

"Has anyone?" I pressed, opening the question to the class, though their answer was the same.

"I don't even think I've ever seen him off that pillow," Suzetta admitted, motioning to the animal's usual spot on the professor's desk.

"Exactly—meaning we can all but rule out his leaving by himself. Though even if he did go of his own accord, I'm sure there was a reason. And I'm sure it was one of *you*."

I looked again at the entry log and its list of names, each one a suspect, each one a potential culprit. But which of them was it? And just how guilty were they?

"Oh, come on, Izra," jeered Bravel. "You expect us to believe that someone in this class is some cold-blooded catnapper?"

"Perhaps," I shrugged, holding his gaze. "I'll find out if so."

He rolled his eyes. "Yeah? And what about you? You're so innocent? I notice you conveniently left your own name off that list."

"Not conveniently," I replied. *"Empirically.* Unlike the six of you, I did not enter this classroom last night, nor any classroom this entire week. I've had a nasty bout of *Shades Flu*, you see, one which has kept me all but locked in my dormitory. Why, for the past three days, I fear I've done nothing but burn all my candles down to their wicks and brighten my every bulb near to bursting."

I shuddered at the recollection. Shades Flu was a common yet loathsome affliction amongst arcanes. Caused by excessive *Shading*, or the use of Shade arcana, the best remedy was reasonably found in all things bright. Of course, my luck being what it was, the sun had been trapped behind an overcast sky for the worst of it, though I'd still done my best. For the past 72 hours, my room had been brighter even than Professor Ludregard's.

"I hadn't noticed," Bravel deadpanned.

The few snickers this comment garnered I ignored. Let them laugh, I thought. I doubted if any of them would be laughing soon.

"Right, well, do take note of this," I said. "Someone in this room is responsible for the disappearance of our dear Darsimeon. Someone in this room is *guilty*. And before next period, I intend to find out *who*."

There were no snickers this time. In fact, the room was as quiet as a corpse. Was the culprit beginning to sweat? I wondered. If they weren't yet, it would not be long. I was on the case, after all. Izra Ravenmott. Head of the class. Captain of the debate team. And on a sleuthing streak to boot.

Say what they might behind my back, shoot me their poisonous looks—it all mattered not. When push came to shove, there were two things no student of Avenwood Academy could deny about Izra Ravenmott.

I'm never wrong. And I never lose.

"Clear the room," I commanded. "I'll conduct interviews individually. That way no one's story will be influenced by another's."

"More like so you can trick us into implicating each other," Bravel spat. "Don't tell her anything!" He roared to the class, nearly capsizing his desk. "She's trying to throw us all to the wolves!"

"Cool it, Blaze," Bronte said. "You know as well as I do that's not Izra's game."

"Thank you, Bronte," I said, feeling a satisfied smile pulling across my lips, though the canine wasn't finished.

"She might be an intense know-all obsessed with being right, but she's not a cheat. She's fair, she's thorough, and most importantly, she has a way of getting to the truth."

"A way, huh?" Bravel rolled his eyes.

"That's right," I said. "Would you like me to demonstrate?"

He met my gaze and waited a moment before allowing his mouth to curl into the tiniest of grins.

"No, that won't be necessary," he answered. And it was an honest answer. Unquestionably honest, and everyone knew it.

By then I was grinning back. That was my edge, after all. The reason I could always tell what everyone was thinking, or what they really meant, anyway. It was my gift. My *aura*. Every student at the academy had one. Every arcane who had ever lived. A special ability unique to the person. Separate from the genres, and defined only by that which had come before. Mine revealed the truth. A question

come from my lips could not be answered dishon-
estly. It could be ignored, yes. Could be dodged
or diverted, but only still to other truths. Never a
lie. Omissions and euphemisms, as close to truth
as they are to falsehood, were rarely excused. No,
when someone spoke to me, they had no choice but
to do so with candor.

I won't say that it has always been a blessing.
There can be cruelty in truth told so bluntly. A
harshness to thoughts and feelings shared always
without filter. It can be oppressive, though I've
learned to adapt. Learned to harden myself to that
knife-edge and turn its sharpness to my advantage.

"Wonderful," I said, clasping my hands together.
"Shall we begin, then? I don't know about you all,
but I'd rather prefer these affairs did *not* extend into
next period. Is that all right with everyone? Yes?
Splendid. We'll start as the log indicates. The first
person to enter the classroom last night was..."

***

"...Bronte B'nitus."

"Izra," the canine said with a nod, and his deep
voice reverberated through the now empty classroom.

We sat across from each other, Ludregard's desk
in between. Despite the professor's chair being
larger and taller than the one Bronte sat in, the

large Dobermann still towered over me. Staring up at him, it was strange to think that the canine was some 14 months my junior.

"What time did you enter the classroom last night?" I asked first.

"'Round nine," he said, and it matched what he'd written in the log sheet.

"Early," I noted, scratching down the same in my journal.

Bronte shrugged. "Figured the sooner I got it done, the sooner I could be getting back to bed."

"Of course. And did it go well?"

"See for yourself," he said, nodding to an item on the desk. It was a crystal ball affixed to a wooden stand. Newly imported from the Southern Isles, we'd been using it to practice *Glowing* all year. Bronte extended his hand toward the ball and it immediately came alight. Previously murky and dim, its innards now shone with white brilliance.

"Impressive," I said, making another note. Bronte had always been adept in the practice of the genres, and he seemed to have a special knack for Glow. Of course, I'm sure I could have done the same or better, though his skill was still worth acknowledging. He was certainly far better than some of our other classmates.

"Tell me about Darsimeon, then. Was he here when you were?"

"Sure was," the canine said with a nod. He gestured to the empty cushion on Ludregard's desk. "Sat right there on his rump the whole time. Watched me like he was bored. Or tired. Knowing that cat, it was probably both."

"He sat right there, did he?" I asked, narrowing my eyes.

"That's right."

When my face didn't change, he frowned. "What, you don't believe me?"

"No, no," I said, touching the end of my pen to my lips. "It's just...well, look at yourself, Bronte. You're tall, you're well-muscled, you're..."

"A big, scary dog?"

"Precisely. And my fear is that—even if you did not intend to—you might have frightened the cat into fleeing anyway. Are you very sure that he was still here, even as you left?"

"Yes," he said, firmly. "Dary was still here, and I remember because I gave him a scratching on my way out. And before you ask, no, the experience wasn't traumatizing for him. Dary knows me, you see. Has gotten to liking me, even. Same as I've gotten to liking him. That's the thing everyone gets wrong about us canines. We don't have no problems with cats. And for the most part, cats don't have no problems with us. Not like they do with our four-legged cousins, anyway. And *felines*, too. Woof. You might ask Sakina how her and her kind get on with the moggies." He brought a hand to the side of his mouth as if to speak discretely. "Not too good, way I hear it." He shrugged. "But that's a natural thing. More to do with biology than actual temperament. You might think the same'd be true of canines, but nah. So long as there's a mutual respect there, we can coexist. Can be friends, even." He paused for a moment, seemed to consider his next words. "Though you can't say that for everyone."

"Oh?"

Bronte shook his head. "Nah. Some people get along with cats like Professor Smud gets along with Professor Ringlot. And ain't no difference in biology got a thing to do with it, neither."

"An interesting observation," I noted. "And a true one, I think. Do you know of anyone like that in particular, Bronte? Perhaps one of our classmates?"

With what I sensed was some hesitation, the canine nodded.

"Tell me."

"Now let me be clear here, Izra. I'm not trying to incriminate nobody."

"Of course."

"I just care about finding out what happened to Dary."

"Of course."

"And since you asked me, I'll be honest."

He had no choice there, but I didn't say as much.

He leaned in close, lowered his voice before saying: "If there's anyone in our class that *doesn't* get on with cats. And doesn't quite care for Dary in particular, it's...

***

"...Bravel Blaze"

"That's me," he grinned, and I could have puked for the sliminess of it.

"Right," I said, not returning the expression. "What time did you take your exam last night?"

He tilted his head back, made a show of trying to remember.

"Pff–" he blew out a puff of air that made the bangs on his forehead jump. "Must've been...oh, ten?"

"Bravel, please, let's not drag this out any longer than we need to."

"Oh, Izra, how your words pierce me," he said, grasping at his chest and feigning hurt. "Are you saying you don't enjoy my company?"

"About as much as Professor Smud enjoys Professor Ringlot's company."

"Ouch," he said through a smile.

"So you arrived at ten for your exam," I repeated, checking that it matched the time in the log. "How did it go?"

For an instant, his smile faltered, though he quickly restored it.

"As well as I expected."

"Mm. And how do you suppose Professor Ludregard will grade it?"

"In accordance with her rubric and the school's standards, of course," he said with a smirk, and I had to give him credit—he was quicker than most, though I was determined.

"What letter grade, Bravel?"

"Why...the same as I got on our last exam."

"Which was?"

"A grade I'll...live with."

"Was it a B?"

He sighed. "Yes, Izra. It was a B. There, I said it. Are you happy now?"

"More than you could ever know," I said, and now it was my turn to smirk. Bravel sneered in return.

"Whatever, Ravenmott. Are you going to ask me about the cat, or can I leave?"

"I'd say your leaving depends on what you *did* with the cat."

"Great," he said, and was already rising from the desk. "Because I didn't do a thing."

"You're sure about that?"

"Uh-huh."

"Darsimeon was here when you came *and* when you left?"

"Yup." He pushed his chair in. "Are we done here?"

"Just one more question, Bravel. Do you *like* cats?"

He narrowed his eyes. "No. As a matter of fact, I don't. What does that have to do with this?"

"Maybe nothing," I said with a shrug. I drew a slow circle in my journal. "Maybe everything..."

"Oh, come on, Izra. You don't like me, fine. But don't try and pin this on me because of it. I'm not special. Plenty of people don't like cats."

"You know that as a statistical truth?"

"No. Dammit! I mean, no, not *statistically*, but I know I'm not the only person that doesn't get on with them. Bronte and Sakina probably hate 'em too."

"You *hate* Darsimeon?"

"No, but I'd say I have much better things to do with my time than dither on about where he went!" He clasped a hand over his mouth, eyes wide at the callousness of his own confession. "Oh, curse that aura of yours! Can't you give it a rest for once?"

"And prevent the truth from coming out?"

"You want the truth? Here's the only one that matters. I can prove I didn't do anything to that cat, because as soon as I was leaving, Suzetta was coming in. She saw the cat was fine. She'll vouch for me!"

I made a final note in my journal and underlined it. "We'll see."

***

"No, Bravel didn't do anything," Suzetta said before noisily blowing her nose into a handkerchief. "I came in just as he was leaving and Darsimeon was right there"—she gestured to the empty cushion on the desk—"same as always."

"And what time was that?"

Suzetta thought for a moment. "Probably close to ten-thirty. That's when I'd planned to arrive for my exam, anyway."

I nodded as it matched the time on the log sheet. "I see. And about your exam, did it go okay?"

"Erm...the second time, yes."

"You took the exam twice?" I asked, raising an eyebrow.

Suzetta's eyes went wide. It seemed she hadn't even realized what she'd said.

"I–yes, I mean...I didn't..." She hesitated, seemed to grasp for some kind of alibi, some way to take it back. But then, realizing it was useless, eventually sighed.

"Listen, I know it's against the rules, but I *had* to, Izra, all right? My first try I was...distracted."

"Distracted?" I asked making a note. "By what?"

Suzetta's brow furrowed then, her small features contorting in pint-sized infuriation. "By some *inconsiderate* person's lights," she said, jabbing a finger at something out the window. Some fifty paces beyond, an adjacent wing of the academy could be seen, uniform windows running across gray stone. It was one of the residence halls.

"I'm sorry...lights?"

"Yes! Lights!" Suzetta cried in a huff. "I don't know if it was a party or some simpleton's idea of a joke, but there was a light shining from one of those windows so bright I could hardly see! Or rather, I *could* see, and that was the problem. Glow exams are supposed to be taken in the dark, you know? Not with a great beacon beside you. It would be like taking a *Burn* exam in a bonfire!"

"So it was the abundance of light that caused you to botch your exam?"

"Er, yes," she said shamefully. "But my second attempt went much smoother!"

"What changed?"

"Why, I closed the blinds, of course. Made it near pitch-black in here. I must say, the difference was quite literally night and day."

"I see," I said, jotting down a few more notes. There was a moment of silence as I finished writing. "Now, about your—"

"Please don't tell Professor Ludregard," Suzetta blurted suddenly, and I realized her eyes were desperate. "Obviously I know it's against the rules to take a second try, but given the circumstances, I really think that I—"

"Don't worry about it," I said, waving a hand. "I won't say anything to her."

Though if she asks me, I'll have no choice but to tell the truth.

"What?"

Suzetta suddenly wore a look of horror, all of her previous relief vanished, and I silently cursed at myself as I realized I'd spoken aloud. Leakage. I shrugged. No choice but to own it now. "If she asks for a report on my findings, I'll need to be honest. And that means *completely* honest."

"I...I understand," she said after a moment, and I felt a pang of guilt at the hurt in her voice. She blew her nose again and readjusted her glasses. "Was there...anything else you needed to know?"

I nodded. "You said Darsimeon was here when you arrived. Was the same true when you left?"

"Well, it was harder to see in the dark, but yes, he was."

"You're sure?"

She nodded. "I remember seeing his eyes. He'd been sleeping before, I think. But as soon as the blinds went down he seemed to wake up. Just sat there, staring at me with those big eyes of his."

"I see. And do you happen to know who took their exam after you?"

"Yes, actually, I believe it was..."

***

"Guyland Creshti, good to meet ya!" the cheery testudine said with a wave. With the crystal ball sat on the desktop between us, I could only see the top of his shell.

"We've known each other for two years, Guyland," I said, shifting the ball so that I could see him clearly. Despite being older than everyone in the class by a number of years, Guyland was still the shortest by a significant margin.

He squinted at me a moment, leaning forward in his chair to get a closer look. "Oh! Izra! It's you!" he exclaimed suddenly, then laughed. "Sorry. These tortoise eyes aren't the strongest."

"That's quite all right," I assured him. "Now tell me, what time did you take your exam last night?"

"Must have been eleven o'clock," he said, bringing an olive-colored hand to his chin. "Yes, must have been eleven."

"Was Darsimeon in the classroom when you arrived?"

"Oh yes. In the classroom and all around it. I daresay the little creature must have been pacing about the entire time. Seemed like something was bothering him, it did. Bothering him bad."

"Interesting," I said, scribbling down the detail. "Any idea what it was?"

The tortoise shook his head. "I can't say. It was very dark here last night, and I'll admit that most of my focus had been on the task at hand."

"Right, your exam. How did it go?"

At this, the tortoise's head lowered some into his shell, and I felt a pang of guilt as I realized who I was talking to. It was common knowledge within the class that Guyland was a *dudder*, an arcane incapable of nearly all genre magic. Worse still, he had yet to discover his aura. Had it not been for his above average proficiency in *Drip* arcana alone, I doubted if he'd have been enrolled in Avenwood at all.

"Well, I suppose it went as well as my exams usually go. About as well as...erm...as well as—uh..." He paused to scratch at his bald, green head. "Hmm, it seems I also struggle with finding the appropriate analogy. Erm, I suppose what I'm trying to say is...that my exam went about as well as—"

"Professor Smud's day goes when he's forced to spend it with Professor Ringlot?"

I watched Guyland's face light up at this, all of his previous embarrassment quickly evaporating. "Yes!" he laughed. "Yes, exactly!"

I allowed myself a smile back. "Right. So, when you left then, was Darsimeon still restless?"

"Mm, yes, if I remember correctly."

"But he was still in the room?"

"Oh, yes. He was most definitely still in the room."

I nodded, tapping my foot lightly as I finished a final note. When I was done, I sighed.

"Guyland, I'm afraid there's a part of your story that isn't adding up."

"I'm...I'm sorry?"

"You've told me that the room was quite dark when you used it. You've also told me that your eyesight is poor. And yet, despite both these things being true, you say you witnessed Darsimeon pacing about the entire time. I'm sorry, but how can that be possible? When you say you *saw* him, do you mean that literally? Or perhaps it's merely what you heard? *And if tortoise ears are as bad as tortoise eyes, can we even trust that?*

He laughed and I realized with a jolt that I'd spoken aloud again.

"Oh, don't worry," he said, tapping at his temple. "You might not be able to see them, but I daresay these tortoise ears are like a fox. Though even if they weren't, I'm confident my testimony would still hold water, for I did actually *see* the critter, as you say, if only his two eyes with mine. They're bright, you know, cat eyes. Just like Sakina's—when she's not, er...*hidden*, of course. No, I assure you, despite the darkness, I saw those big orbs of his bobbing about clear as day. Darsimeon was here. As I came and as I left."

"Hm," I intoned, adding another note. "And you didn't see anything else?"

"Nothing at all."

***

"Rula Yotenza."

"Hey, Izra," said the red-haired girl before me, and her smile was as genuine as it was pretty. I didn't return it.

"What time did you take your exam last night?"

In an instant, that pretty, freckle-surrounded smile vanished, was replaced with pursed lips and a furrowed brow. After staring hard at the desk for a while, Rula's gaze finally returned, her expression dopey. "I don't remember."

"You don't remember."

"It was late, I know that," she said, nodding slowly, trying to piece it together. "Much later than I'm usually up."

"You put eleven-thirty on the log sheet. Does that ring a bell?"

"Yes!" she said immediately, her smile instantly returned. "Yes, it was eleven-thirty for sure."

My eyes narrowed. Something about her rapid certainty wasn't convincing. "And if I said you'd put down eleven-forty-five instead?"

Again, her smile quickly vanished, brows knitting in confusion. She looked up opaquely. "Did I put both?"

"What? No, you—" I shook my head. "Nevermind. When you arrived for your exam last night, was Darsimeon in the classroom?"

"Dar...simeon?"

"That's right."

She began to nod, and then: "Who is Darsimeon?"

I blinked.

"The cat?" I made a motion to the empty cushion on the professor's desk, and only then did clarity dawn.

"Oh!" she exclaimed, smiling again. She pointed to the empty cushion herself. "The professor's cat!"

Oh dear.

I took a moment to sigh before responding. "Yes, the cat that is currently missing. Was he in the room last night when you arrived?"

At this, Rula's gaze returned to the same spot on her desk, forehead wrinkling in what seemed to be deep concentration as she tried to remember. She remained this way for a long time. So long, in fact, that I considered asking a different question. Just as I was about to, however, she unfroze.

"Yes," she said finally, and though her expression still seemed somewhat vacuous, something in her voice told me that she was sure. "He was right by the door." She pointed her finger to the spot. "I remember because I had to stop him from running out into the hall."

"He was trying to leave?"

Rula nodded. "It was all I could do to contain him. Much faster than he looks, that one. And then he was just pacing about the entire room. Seemed nervous, the poor thing—though I doubt if the extra steps weren't good for him." She lowered her voice and looked around before adding: "He's a bit tubby, don't you think?"

"Well, I suppose but—" I caught myself. "Oh, nevermind that. So you say you *did* manage to keep him inside the classroom?"

"Yes."

"And then when you left, did he try to leave again?"

"About as quickly as Professor Smud leaves a room when Professor Droven walks in," Rula said, smirking to herself. I didn't bother to correct her.

"And did you contain him that time as well?"

"Of course."

I hesitated, pen against my lips. "And you remembered to close the door behind you?"

Rula laughed. "Oh, come on, Izra. I'm not *that* forgetful."

I nodded. "What time did you leave?"

Her face went blank. "I forgot."

"Right," I said, making another note. "Tell me, Rula, is there anything else you *do* remember from last night? You mentioned that Darsimeon tried to leave, that he was pacing, but was there anything more? Anything else that struck you as odd? Out of the ordinary? *Suspicious?*"

"Let me think," she said, tapping a finger on her chin as she tilted her head back. And think she did, for as good and long a while as she had thought prior. I waited until a full minute had passed before deciding to call it.

"If there wasn't anything, it's—"

"No," she said suddenly, her blue eyes sharp as they turned on me. "I remember now. There *was* something strange."

I flipped to a new page in my journal. "Tell me."

"Well, on my way back from the exam, I stopped by Torrin's room." Her eyes dropped at this admission, a bright red hue filling her freckled cheeks. "Of course, I wasn't going there for any *particular* reason. It's just...well, I have to pass his room to get to mine, is all. You know how it is in the residence halls. You're neighbors with Sakina, right?"

"I am."

"Exactly! You get it. Well, anyways, I knew he also had to take his exam, so I figured I'd just stop by and let him know that the room was open." She began to twirl a strand of hair around her finger. "Of course, I would have done the same for anyone. It's not like I wanted to talk to Torrin specifically. It's just that he's my neighbor and—"

"I get it. Keep going."

"Right, well, I knocked on his door and he answered it looking as good as he usually does, only...something was different."

"Rula, if you're going to tell me that he bought a new cloak or changed his hair or something then I really don't—"

"No, no, nothing like that," she said, shaking her head. "I promise it's important." She paused. "Though it did have to do with his cloak."

I rolled my eyes. "Fine. What?"

"Well, Torrin is always very well put together, as I'm sure you've noticed. Well dressed, well groomed, never a hair out of place. Only, last night was different. Last night, there were more like a *hundred* hairs out of place.

"I'm sorry...*hairs*?"

"That's right. He was covered in them. All the way down the front of his cloak he had them, these tiny little hairs. And it wasn't *his* hair, either." She shook her head resolutely. "No, his hair is much darker than whatever *those* were."

"So he had hair on him," I said flatly. "Sorry, but I'm failing to see how that's relevant." I flashed the tiniest of grins. "Perhaps Torrin simply found himself a new girlfriend."

"What?" Rula said, horrified. "No, no, that couldn't be it."

"No way of knowing for sure," I said with a shrug. I decided to tease her a little more. "Think about it logically. If you're so sure it wasn't his own hair he was covered in, then it had to be someone else's, right?"

"No, Izra, you don't understand," Rula said firmly. "It wasn't *human* hair he was covered in. It was *cat* hair."

***

"Torrin Jesseranda."

"Izra," Torrin replied with a nod. The young man was dressed all in black, his bright, handsome eyes shining smartly beside dark locs. As he crossed his arms before me, I could not help but notice the abundance of hair that covered his sleeves.

"What time did you take your exam last night?"

He took a moment to recollect. "'Round two."

"Quite late," I commented, making a note. The time matched that which he'd written on the log sheet, though it was a full two hours after Rula had left.

"I'm a night owl," Torrin replied with a shrug.

"I see. Tell me, did Rula stop by your room last night?"

"Rula? Yeah, she came by a bit earlier in the night. Let me know that the room was open after she'd taken her exam."

"But you didn't leave then?"

"No." He shook his head and then smiled. "No, I was a bit preoccupied."

"With?"

Torrin considered for a moment. "You know, it'd probably be easier just to show you." He pulled something out of his cloak and set it on the desk. My eyes widened. It was Darsimeon.

"Izra, meet Wiggelin."

"Ah—who?"

"My little friend here," he said, giving the cat a scratch on the head, and as it purred its satisfaction, I realized suddenly that it was not Darsimeon, but another cat entirely. Very similar in coat, but much smaller. Just a kitten.

"His name is Wiggelin," Torrin repeated. "Newest member of the Jesseranda clan."

"I...see," I said, still marvelling at the kitten's resemblance to Darsimeon. I made a note. "I suppose that would explain the cat hair?"

"Oh yeah," he laughed, dusting himself off in a way that made little difference. "Ol' Wiggy here's quite the shedder." He brought a hand to one side of his mouth. "Quite the urinator too, though we've been working on doing that in the right place." He moved to scratch the kitten behind its ear. "Haven't we, Wiggy?"

The kitten let out a tiny meow in reply and I had to smile.

"Do you often carry him around in your cloak with you?"

"Lately, yeah," Torrin said with a nod. "He gets a bit anxious if I'm away for too long, and I think the anxiety might trigger the bladder, so at least until we've got the whole potty training thing sorted, I figured it best he stays with me."

"Makes sense," I nodded. "So was he with you when you came to the classroom last night?"

"He was."

"And what about Darsimeon?"

"No, by the time I came in, Dary was gone."

My pen froze mid-note. "At two o'clock, you mean?"

Torrin nodded. "The door was open when I came in and he was gone from his usual spot"—he gestured to the cushion on the professor's desk—"but I didn't think anything of it. Figured Ludregard must've taken him out for the night...maybe so we could do our exams, I don't know." He shook his head. "I should've known something was up. Dary's never not here."

"You're certain he wasn't anywhere else in the room?" I asked, jotting more notes down as I spoke. "It would've been as dark as it gets by that hour. And other students mentioned that Darsimeon had been pacing about. Is there any chance he could have been tucked away in a corner somewhere and you just didn't notice?"

Torrin shook his head. "No, no I..." he hesitated. He was hiding something.

"What?" I pressed.

"Well I uh...I lit the room up pretty good with my exam." He scratched at the back of his head modestly. "Light that bright, I would've seen him."

It was his truth, though I pursed my lips at it. *If his Glowing is anything like his Burning, then it couldn't have been* that *bright.*

"My Glowing's actually gotten a bit better," he said, and I realized with horror that I'd spoken my inner thoughts aloud again. Torrin raised his palm toward the crystal ball, and in an instant it was shining brightly. "See?"

"Yes, that's, ah...very good," I faltered, still aware of the heat that had risen in my face.

"So yeah, Dary definitely wasn't here," Torrin repeated. "I'm sure of it. If not for the Glowing then for this little one," he said, ruffling the hair on Wiggelin's back. "Cats, they've got a way of sensing each other, you know? No way could Darsimeon have been here and Wiggy not known it." He shook his head. "Like a lynx, this one. You know, I bet we could even show you. Hey, Wiggy," he said, poking the kitten lightly. When it turned to face him, Torrin grinned. "Is there a *cat* in here, buddy?" he asked, putting extra emphasis on the word. "Where's the *cat*? Find the *cat*."

For a moment, Wiggelin sniffed at the air, turning his head to observe the room with an acuity impressive for his age. Then, with a swiftness equally as impressive, he leapt from the desk, nimbly bounding from one top to the next until he was at the other end of the classroom, and all in a matter of seconds. He stopped at the very last desk in the far corner. From there, he seemed to stare directly at the back wall.

Mow, came his fledgling meow.

"Oh well, he's still a kitten," Torrin said, already rising to retrieve him. He gave Wiggelin another scratch on the head before bundling him within the folds of his cloak. "We'll keep working on it. But yeah, that's about it for my experience last night. Was there anything else, Izra?"

"No," I said, and my eyes were still on that last desk in the far corner. "No, I believe I have everything I need."

***

A little while later it was complete: the sum total of my notetaking and questioning plastered all across the class chalkboard. I had all the data, all the details, all of the precious little cogs that make a mystery tick. Because they do tick, even the worst of them—like clockwork.

I paused to let a shiver rack through me, then sighed. It seemed at least a few symptoms of my recent affliction were still lingering. I took a moment to turn the room's lights up even brighter. You'd think a Glow classroom, of all places, would be the best remedy for one suffering from Shades Flu. Though even with the overheads shining at their brightest and the windows streaming sunlight, I longed for the superior illumination of my dorm room. So brilliantly had I lit the place, I wouldn't be surprised if it had been visible from the moon.

Just get to the bottom of it, I told myself. *The quicker this mystery is solved, the quicker we can all get back to our lives. Not that my life comprises much* besides *the solving of mysteries lately, but nevertheless.*

I paused a moment, taking stock of the empty room and considering whether or not I'd spoken the last of my thoughts aloud. Again, I found my gaze pulling to that final desk in the back corner, a grin curling its way onto my lips. Suddenly, I could not wait to get started.

As always, I began aloud.

"Six different suspects. Six different stories. One detective. One missing cat." I turned to face the chalkboard. "Where do they connect? Where do they contradict? How does each piece fit itself into the whole?"

I moved to the first desk in the first row, where a certain, well-muscled canine sat. "We start with Bronte. He arrives at nine, and for all intents and purposes, he's the stereotypical suspect. Who but a big, scary dog to be responsible for scaring off a cat? Another school, another set of circumstances, why, it would be textbook. But not here. Ironic as it sounds, Bronte might just be the least suspicious of our suspects. Darsimeon remained long after the canine's departure, and the two's kinship is well-known by many."

I moved to the next desk in the row, the middle- and front-most of the entire room. Perhaps the most detestable seat in any class, it was commonly reserved for brownnosers and non-literal teacher's pets. Call me judgemental, but I'd been in enough classrooms to know. The student who sat in this seat was usually either socially inept or a pompous blowhard. And, in the case of this class, he was both.

"Bravel Blaze," I said, careful not to make actual physical contact with his desk lest I contract some kind of disease. "A confessed cat-hater, he certainly has motive. And if personal character is anything to be considered in a case such as this, his certainly doesn't bode well." I pursed my lips, trying hard at the logic before eventually giving it up to sigh. "Unfortunately, much like Bronte, the present evidence exonerates him. Darsimeon was seen safe and sound in the hours after he left, and Suzetta even vouched for him. Of course, there's a possibility that he returned later in the night, though that could be said for anyone, and with nothing to prove it, a possibility it must remain."

The third desk was the last of the front row, right beside the window. There was a spare handkerchief folded neatly on its top.

"Suzetta Insperenza comes third. Arrives at ten-thirty and can't focus. There is a light, she claims, shining so brightly from outside the window that it disrupts her first try at the exam and she's forced to take another. A clear violation of test procedures, though she claims it was appropriate. I wonder, was that the only rule she felt justified in breaking?" I took a moment to peer out the window, eyeing the adjacent wing whence such blinding lights had allegedly came, and frowned. "Hard to believe there were many parties going on last night. And even if there had been, could they have produced such a light as to disturb someone so far beyond it?" After a long minute of consideration, I decided I was not sure. "It changes little either way. Darsimeon was seen later in the night, and so despite her curious testimony, the evidence fairs Suzetta the same as the rest."

I moved to the next row of desks, still by the third, closest to the window. This one was covered in an array of pencil sketches and other scribbles.

"Guyland Creshti next. Small means, smaller motive, and perhaps the smallest chance of making a quick getaway." I slid into the testudine's seat and was surprised to find purchase much sooner than expected. I'd forgotten that his chair sat a little higher than the rest, a necessity should the small tortoise have wanted to see anything besides the backs of his classmate's heads.

"Doesn't exactly look the part of a cat-napper, but then, looks can be deceiving. I wonder, did Guyland's eyes deceive him, when he says he saw Darsimeon's? And what's to be made of the pacing? In all the time I've known this classroom's cat, I've barely seen him move at all, let alone pace." I drummed my fingers along the desktop. "It's a key detail—perhaps *the* key detail, though its significance eludes me. What exactly caused Darsimeon to become so restless? What changed between Suzetta and Guyland's exams? Was it something one of them did? Was it something already done?" I looked at the collection of empty desks, each one as practically identical as the last, and sighed. There were too many questions. Too many uncertainties. The facts remained: Darsimeon was still in the room following Guyland's departure. So, at least for the time being, the testudine appeared innocent too. Onto the next.

"Rula Yotenza," I said, perching myself atop the redhead's desk. It was right beside Guyland's.

"Nothing hidden in her testimony. No lies, no half-truths, and nothing omitted. Yes, more so than any other student, I'm sure that everything Rula told me was the full, unadulterated truth. Unfortunately, her words may still be the least reliable." I took a moment to picture Rula's pretty, clueless face and sighed. If only my aura had the ability to root out confusion. Misrememberings and misunderstandings. Get to the actual truth, even if someone believed fervently in a falsehood. Regrettably, such power was beyond my scope. So long as someone was truly convinced of what they were telling me, my aura would not contradict them. *Even if they don't know their left from their right.*

I peered down at Rula's desk and spotted a crudely-drawn heart carved into its surface. Rula and Torrin's names had been etched within it, only Torrin's had been misspelled in two places. I sighed again.

"Whatever had been bothering Darsimeon during Guyland's exam had escalated enough by Rula's to have him wanting to flee the room. She says she kept him in, but can her recollection be trusted? And what of Torrin's finding the door open? Was that Rula's doing? Her forgetfulness has certainly done worse. Could this entire mystery boil down to a simple lapse in attention? A door left ajar and a cat with opportunity?" I eyed the journal pages stuck upon the chalkboard, trying to see something in them I'd missed before. The longer I looked, however, the more defined each dead end seemed to become.

Except for one, of course.

I moved to the next desk in sequence. "Last but not least comes Torrin Jesseranda. Torrin and Wiggelin, that is. The boy and the kitten arrive to find the door open and Darsimeon gone, making Torrin the only student to have not seen the professor's cat last night." I chewed my lip, thinking, thinking.

"He comes well after midnight, a full two hours following Rula's departure, making the exact time of Darsimeon's leaving hard to pinpoint. Did he go immediately after Rula? Later? Did another student return and take him in the time between? And at what point was the door opened?"

Questions, questions, and questions. They seemed to pile before me like the kitten hair strewn across Torrin's desk. Each one unique yet ambiguous, jumbling together until it was all just a heap of gray.

Though was there not a red thread among them?

Just a hunch, I told myself. Just a hunch, though the more I looked upon those empty desks, the clearer vindication seemed to appear on the horizon. There were three seats I'd yet to examine. The first, of course, was my own, leftmost of the last row by the window. The second, middle of the last row, belonged to Osric Garrowind. Osric was currently on holiday in the northlands, and so, much like me, had not been in class—or even on school grounds—all week. The third and final desk was the rightmost of the last row. The far desk in the corner. It was the desk that belonged to Sakina Graychild. It was the desk Wiggelin had beelined for, when Torrin had told him to find a cat, and it was the desk I'd been staring at ever since.

"You can drop the veil, Sakina. I know you're there."

For a moment, there was nothing. Nothing but silence. And it was a silence so perfectly unrelenting that another might have judged me mad for doubting it, though I didn't waver. I knew well when I was onto something. And it did not take long for that something to appear.

From the emptiness of the desk, something began to materialize. Thin shadows, previously inconceivable, slowly began to darken, to lengthen, and to take shape into something thicker. It was a dim something at first, enshrouded in a smoky, swirling haze of Shade arcana. Though where the magic of shadows usually appeared as black as ink, the color of this thing was unmistakably gray. A moment later, it was clear. The smoke dissipated, and the formless became familiar. Something tall and slender now sat in that last desk, something with its legs and arms crossed quite casually. Something with a long, gray tail.

"Hello Sakina," I said, nodding to the feline before me.

"Hello Izra," she said, nodding back. Her eyes were a pair of glowing yellow lanterns. Her grin a sawtooth knife. "What gave me away?"

"I had suspicions from the beginning," I said, turning back to the chalkboard. "When I saw your name missing from the log sheet, of course. And then when I noticed your desk—so gray on such a sunny day. Your *shrouding* is good, Sakina, by far the best in our class, though Wiggelin was not fooled."

"Pesky four-legger," she sneered. "I'd noticed Torrin had a new scent on him lately. The furball explains it."

"Will he be the next cat you make disappear, then?"

Sakina's grin returned at this. It was long and thin and curled at her cheeks. "You think *I* was responsible for Darsimeon?"

"Of course," I said with a nod. "All the evidence points to it."

Sakina laughed at this, and she rose from her desk, seemed to *float* from it, that shadowy smoke returning just long enough to enshroud her, and to pull her, ghost-like, through its front where she appeared again, now sitting cross-legged on its top.

"You're a smart girl, Izra, but your detective skills need work. It's my opinion that the *evidence* points to someone else entirely."

"Someone else?" I echoed, raising my eyebrows. "And who would that be?"

Sakina's grin grew wider, curling tighter at her cheeks as two fangs sprouted underneath. "Let's have another look at our suspects, shall we?"

She disappeared in a puff of smoke, leaving only faint traces of gray across the room before reappearing at its front, perched now atop Bronte's desk.

"Bronte B'nitus," she said, mimicking my own intonation. "The big canine adores the classroom cat. Surely, he must be innocent, right?"

I nodded. "No evidence points to his being guilty."

"Maybe not, though other details he shared may point to something else, no?" Sakina took a moment to examine the desk she sat in, flicking her tail against either side of it before looking up again. "Bronte said his exam went well, yes? Lit up the room nice and bright, did he?"

"That's what he said."

"And Bravel..." Sakina continued, shifting, in a pillar of smoke, from the top of Bronte's desk to the top of Bravel's, "...he did the same?"

I shrugged. "Supposedly."

"Oh, come now," Sakina said, dropping her head to one side. "We both know he's as talented as he is insufferable. Can we not give him credit for both?"

"He only got a B."

"Which, I'd remind you, is still a grade that reflects mastery."

"Whatever," I said, rolling my eyes.

"Good. So, here's what we know. Our first two examinees light up the room like a holiday pine tree. And all the while, Darsimeon sleeps safe and sound." She shifted her gaze to the next desk. "Then what happens?"

"Suzetta botches her first exam."

"Why?"

"She was distracted," I recite. "She claims a light from outside interfered with her Glowing."

"Outside."

I nodded. "From the residence hall," I said, motioning to the adjacent wing out the window. "Presumably, from a party."

"Presumably," Sakina echoed, taking a moment to gaze out the window herself before turning back. "And then?"

"And then she takes the exam again. This time with the blinds closed."

"A critical detail, and not the only one Suzetta gave us," the feline said, stretching herself out across the window sill. "Unlike the conclusion of

Bronte and Bravel's exams, by the end of Suzetta's, Darsimeon is awake."

I took a moment to consider. It was true that Suzetta was the first to have described Darsimeon's eyes as being open, though how exactly that was a 'critical detail', I had no clue.

The shadows engulfed the feline again, sucked her into their rippling reserves only to spit her out again on the other side of the room, on top of the fourth desk in sequence.

"Little Dary is still up during Guyland's exam. Up and pacing, or so it's told. What say you of this?"

I pursed my lips. "Well, I believe Guyland was true in his assessment; something must have been bothering him."

"Yes, yes," Sakina said, nodding in agreement. She stroked her chin with a long finger. "But what? Perhaps it was Guyland himself?"

I pictured the testudine's wide, friendly face and had to laugh. I found it hard to believe that anything would be put off by his presence. Even if he wasn't already an herbivore.

"Fat chance. Guyland's never scared a thing. Least of all Darsimeon."

Again, Sakina nodded. "And what else do we know about the affable tortoise?"

I considered. "Well, besides Drip magic, his arcane aptitude is negligible. He's a practical dudder."

"And has this influenced your investigation?"

"Not particularly. If anything, I'd say it helps his case."

"So you believe he's innocent?"

"As innocent as the rest of them," I said, gesturing once more to the room of empty desks. "There's no evidence against him."

"Maybe not, though is that your only conclusion?" Sakina's tail wavered slowly, back and forth behind her head. "Is there no more to be gleaned?"

I crossed my arms. "You tell me."

The feline grinned. "Well, knowing what we do about the testudine's arcane ability, what can we assume about his exam performance? Or, better yet, what do we know?"

"He didn't do well."

"Not well at all," Sakina agreed, shaking her head. "Which, of course, tells us what about the ambience of the room?"

"It was...dark?"

"Precisely," Sakina hissed, springing suddenly to the top of another desk. "Not only was it dark, but it was darker than it had ever *been*." Without moving, smoke enveloped her and she reappeared at the window. "With the closed blinds cutting off any light from outside,"—she threw them down with a flourish—"and Guyland's arcane ineptitude similarly eliminating any from within,"—she appeared by the lightswitch and flicked it off—"it was around eleven o'clock, then, that Professor Ludregard's

Glow classroom found itself uncharacteristically *dim*."

I found myself observing the darkened classroom with a strange appreciation. Sakina was right. It *was* unlike the Glow room to be so without light. Perhaps it was simply because I'd spent the past week Shades-ill, sweltering under the combined brightness of every lamp and candle I owned, but even with what small sunlight managed to sneak through the slits in the blinds, something about the classroom being so dark was peculiar, almost...unnatural. To think that it would have been even blacker in the dead of night was a strange wonder indeed.

"So it was dark," I said, using a *Gust* of wind to throw the blinds back open. Sunlight poured onto the unsuspecting feline, making her squint. "That explains what happened to Darsimeon...how, exactly?"

"Let us look to the next piece of evidence," she said, shifting, in shadows, to the fifth desk in sequence. "By the time Rula took her exam, Darsimeon was actively trying to escape the classroom." She rested her head in her hand. "The question is...did he?" She turned to the chalkboard, to my messy diorama of notes and pages, and squinted at it hard before turning back. "I think so."

"Okay. And what exactly is the *evidence* which proves that? Rula says she kept him in."

"Yes, but *did* she?"

"You doubt her testimony?"

"You don't?"

When I didn't respond right away, Sakina rotated on the desk, turned so that she lay on her stomach and began to slowly kick her legs behind. "Rula's a nice girl, though she can be somewhat...shall we say, *absentminded?*" She spotted the heart engraving in the corner of the desk and traced its outline with a clawed finger. "Why, unless it involves a cute boy, I'd say her recollection is all but useless, wouldn't you agree? Surely, she's capable of forgetting to close a door, and also of forgetting that she forgot!"

I found myself chewing on my inner cheek. It was certainly hard to argue. Rula's memory was about as reliable as Guyland's arcana. "So what, you think Rula forgot to close the door, and Darsimeon simply left after that?"

Sakina shrugged. "If it was as dark as we've established it was, it would've been easy to miss, even if Rula *had* remembered the door."

"Oh, well isn't that convenient?" I said, smiling without mirth. "I suppose someone in your position would be partial to that conclusion, you who are a prime suspect. No one was at fault! The cat merely left on his own! Nevermind he's never left this classroom a day of his life. Nevermind that it still doesn't explain *your* absence last night."

"Now, now, Izra, you didn't let me finish." She shifted to Torrin's desk. "I believe we were just speaking of a cute boy?" She took a moment to examine the desktop and all the kitten hair that littered it. She picked up a piece and studied it closely. "Yes, well, I believe we both saw through that red herring, didn't we?" She blew the hair away. "He's innocent."

"Just like the rest of them," I agreed. "And seeing as myself and Osric were both away, that only leaves one possible culprit. You." I sat atop the nearest desk and crossed my legs. "So how about it, Graychild. Why don't you explain *your* whereabouts last night?"

"Happily," she said. Then her eyes narrowed. "Just as soon as you explain yours."

"I'm *sorry?*"

"Where were you last night?" she demanded.

"I—? Well, I was in my room, of course!"

"And you had all the lights on?"

"I did, but—"

"How many lights? Were any of them *Glow*-powered?"

"Twelve total. Eight electrics, two Glowers, and two hybrids." I said automatically, then clamped my hand over my mouth before I said anything more. *Blasted leakage! What am I doing telling her all this? And who does she think she is to be asking me so? I'm the one who's supposed to be asking the questions here!*

"Yes, yes, of course," Sakina replied with a grin. "Though if you ask all the questions, who will know *your* answers?"

When I failed to respond, the feline laughed.

"Oh, don't look so astonished. Did you truly think it was some great secret? Your aura exposes the *truth*, Izra. You ask me a question, and I cannot lie. Though I ask you a question, and neither can you."

And there it was. What I'd thought was my best kept secret. My greatest weakness inside my greatest strength. My arcane irony, my *leakage*, laid out in front of me like a bad joke. I wanted to protest. To deny her words and come up with a hundred retorts. But I couldn't. What she'd said was the truth, after all. To refuse it would be to lie. And for me, just like she'd said, that was impossible.

"Okay, and what of it?" I said, crossing my arms in an attempt at nonchalance. "Ask as many questions as you want. You'll find no guilt in my truths."

"Of course not. Though I wonder..." Sakina went up in smoke again, and this time reappeared right in front of me, those great yellow eyes of hers mere inches from mine, "...what *are* your truths?"

"Like I said," I replied, unwavering beneath those boring lanterns, "you need but ask."

"Fine. But first, tell me, are you feeling better? Has the Shades Flu run its course?"

I nodded.

"Wonderful," she said, her smile somewhat genuine. "Perhaps now we can *both* get some sleep."

"I'm sorry?"

"Glow lamps are powerful things, Izra, as I'm sure you know. Because they run off arcana rather than electricity, they shine much brighter than the mechanical bulb. In fact, were you to light one bright enough, you could even shine it through a wall! Not a thick wall, of course, but a thin one, definitely. Take the walls that separate our dorm rooms, for instance. Yes, paper thin, those ones are. Light a single Glower on one side, and I'm positive its illumination would permeate the other." Her eyes met mine then, and her neutral expression melted into a frown. "Light four at once, and I'm afraid the effect is somewhat overwhelming."

"Are you saying my Glow lights were shining through the walls?"

"Through the walls, and into my room," the feline said with a nod.

"And I take it this disturbed you?" I said, raising an eyebrow.

"Oh, only my slumber, serenity, and quietude."

"Hm," I said, pursing my lips. "Well, Elaina Rubeforde didn't make any complaints,"—this was my neighbor on the alternate side from Sakina—"and she lives just a wall away as well."

"Elaina Rubeforde is as blind as a bat, even by human-standards," Sakina said, waving a hand to dispel the notion. She tapped a single finger to her temple. "Cat eyes are more sensitive to that kind of thing. More perceptive."

"I see. And did it ever occur to you to simply ask me to dim them?"

"As accommodating as I'm sure you would have been to *that* particular request, the opportunity had passed. By the time I realized the source of my disturbed slumber, the night had come for our examinations, and I'd planned to stay up anyway."

"All right then, so what's your point?"

"Getting to it, my dear neighbor. Watch closely."

She vanished again and reappeared at the chalkboard in a plume of gray. "I arrived at one," she said, grabbing a piece of chalk and inserting the time into those already recorded. "After Rula but before Torrin. Darsimeon was gone, and the door was wide open."

"Oh, sure," I said with a snort. "And I suppose you conveniently forgot to sign in?" I asked, gesturing to the log sheet.

"Exactly right, detective. It seems my many nights of disturbed slumber had finally caught up with me. Why, I'd barely sat down at my desk before fatigue overtook me and I dozed off within it. There I remained for the rest of the night, asleep through

Torrin's exam, through the sunrise, and awakening only as you began your questioning this morning."

"You were sleeping," I repeated, unconvinced. "And you were..." I made a twirling motion with my hand, attempting to refer to her smoky, arcana cloak, "...*hidden* the entire time?"

"Call it a defense mechanism," she said with a shrug. "An arcane natural instinct."

"I don't believe you."

"You think I lie to you?" she asked, eyes dancing. I hated that I knew she wasn't. I'd had enough of her games. It was time to get to the truth.

"Did you do anything to Darsimeon?" I demanded.

"No."

"Was he truly gone when you arrived?"

"Yes."

"And you know nothing more of the others questioned?"

"I don't."

"The rest of the class is innocent?"

"The rest of it, yes."

Truth, truth, and truth again! Blasted confounding mystery! This was not how it was supposed to go. The truth was supposed to solve the case, not leave it as cold as it started. I slammed my palms down on the desk before me.

"Well isn't that just splendid? Tell me, Sakina, since you seem to have all the answers, what am

I to make of this? If you're innocent, and Bronte's innocent, and Bravel, Suzetta, Guyland, Rula, and Torrin are too, then what happened? What made Darsimeon leave the classroom last night? Why has he not returned now? What, for goodness sake, is the key to this mystery?"

At my sudden intensity, the feline only smiled. "Let me show you."

"Excuse me?" I started, though before I could even finish the thought, Sakina seized my wrist and pulled me, with surprising strength, off my desk and out the door. Suddenly we were in the hallway, half-running, half-sprinting through the steepled corridors of the academy.

"Sakina!" I exclaimed. "What in the blazes are you doing? What's the meaning of this?" I tried to pull away from her grip, tried to slow our pace, though the feline held fast, and moved faster, forcing me to keep up. Yellow, cat eyes focused ahead, she replied to me without looking.

"Think about it, Izra. If there's one thing we can presume about a cat that's spent most of its life in a Glow classroom, it's that he probably doesn't like the dark."

We turned a corner and found ourselves in a first year hall, where droves of the smaller, brighter-eyed students stopped what they were doing to look up at us with curiosity. No doubt they were wondering—much like myself—what in the world was happening. Sakina did not slow her pace. In fact, as we bobbed and weaved between many a body and book stack, the gray feline actually seemed to speed up.

"Look at the evidence and it proves as much," she continued, carrying on as calmly as if we'd still been sitting in the classroom. "When Bronte and Bravel take their exams, lighting up the room nice and bright, Darsimeon slumbers on without a care. However, when Suzetta and Guyland follow, the room gets darker, and stays darker. Suddenly, kitty wants out."

We were passing faculty rooms now, still at a pace far surpassing that which I would have ever dared alone. Unfortunately, Sakina did not share my prudence. As we dashed past Professor Smud's office, I heard his voice call out into the hall behind us.

"No running in the corridors, Ms. Graychild! You too, Ms. Ravenmott!"

"Oh, let them be, Smud," came another voice from an adjacent office—who but Professor Ringlot? "They're just being kids."

"Kids fitting to run an old man over! They're cretins!"

"Oh, give it a rest, you old crumb..."

We were out of earshot before I could hear anything more.

"Then Rula comes in," Sakina resumed, taking advantage of the less crowded hallway to turn back and look at me as she ran. "And she leaves the door wide open."

"Allegedly," I managed to interject, trying my best to slow our pace by pulling back a bit, though Sakina only pulled forward harder.

"Sure, sure. *Allegedly.* And, if a cat *allegedly* afraid of the dark were to have *allegedly* escaped a dark room, where do you think he *allegedly* would have went?"

I rolled my eyes. "Somewhere brighter, I suppose?"

"Yes! Precisely! And where, pray tell, would that have been?"

"I don't know...the cafeteria? Professor Ludregard's suite? Can we *please* slow down?"

"Not yet!" Sakina cried. Her fangs were beaming now. "We're nearly there! Those were good guesses, but believe me when I say that there was an even brighter place than those last night. The single brightest place in all of Avenwood. A place bright enough to disturb Suzetta's exam a courtyard away, and my slumber right next door."

She halted suddenly. "Ah, here it is."

We'd stopped in the third year residence hall, in front of a door I'd seen many times before. It was my own.

"My dormitory?" I said, squinting at the number and nameplate to be sure I was correct. "I don't understand," I said, shaking my head as I turned back to Sakina. "What exactly are you getting at?"

"You'll see." She pointed to the doorknob. "If you would?"

Grudgingly, I inserted my key and undid the latch, opening the door to my large, still very bright, room. Having spent the better part of the last week as my Shades Flu sanatorium, a few things were understandably out of place. However, aside from the disheveled sheets, the scattered lanterns, and even the hordes of used handkerchiefs, one thing stood out even more peculiarly than the rest.

There on my bed, basking in the combined glow of sun and lamp light, was Darsimeon.

Upon our entrance, he seemed to awake from slumber, opened his eyes and gave a single, careless meow before rolling over and returning to rest. I could hardly believe my eyes. And as I stared, slack-jawed in disbelief, Sakina laughed.

"And just like that, the mystery of the missing cat is solved," she said, crossing her arms and leaning against the door frame. "Taken by the very detective tasked with his finding. What a twist."

I spun around in horror. "No," I protested, wanting to say more—a million things—but finding myself at an utter loss for words. "No, it wasn't...I didn't—"

"Tell it to Professor Ludregard," Sakina said, waving a hand to cut me off. She was already turning to leave. "And do me a favor, later on this evening, when it's lights out...make sure that your lights *are* out." She shot me a wink, and in a billow of gray, vanished.

THE PRETENDER

We were deep in the old Mora Caves when I noticed it. Three packs where there should have been four. We'd put them down to rest up a few minutes before starting our next descent, and it was somewhere in that time when it must have found us.

Saren was about to make a move for one of the packs when I stopped her.

"Wait!" I shouted, loud enough to make her freeze, and the other two turn their heads.

"What?" she asked, confused.

"Don't pick that up," I said, looking around the space we inhabited, searching desperately for a fourth pack.

"Um, okay," she said, slowly returning her hand to her side. She narrowed her eyes at me. "What are you looking for?"

"The fourth pack," I said, still searching. It was dark in the cave, and my headlamp danced in erratic patterns. "Does anyone see it?"

Drake and Gracie were up now too, were standing beside Saren and staring at me with the same confused expression. "The fourth pack?" Drake repeated, and he cast a quick glance around the perimeter of the space. It being a small chamber, a glance was really all that was needed. "I didn't think there was a fourth pack, was there?"

"Yes," I said with a nod, still looking, though the truth was settling in now, was becoming unavoidable. Still I searched. Still I tried to convince myself otherwise. "There had to have been."

"What are you talking about, Fiona?" Gracie asked, and she met my gaze with concern. "You're scaring me."

Finally, I stopped, let out a breath that did little to soothe my nerves. I felt bad for scaring the others, but I was scared too. I tightened my jaw and forced myself to calm.

"Think about it," I said, turning to the three of them. They stood in a line, their headlamps shining back at me from three different heights. "What's the first rule of caving?"

"Never pee in a pothole?" Drake asked.

"The other first rule of caving."

"Never dive without a pack," Saren said.

"Exactly." I nodded. "So if there are four of us,"—I turned my head to the now ominous looking packs on the cavern floor—"why are there only three of them?"

Now Drake was frowning. "Did somebody forget one?"

"Impossible," I said. "It's the first rule."

"Okay, well then who didn't have one?"

A long moment passed in silence, during which everyone considered, thinking back, and thinking hard. Eventually, Saren spoke for us all.

I can't remember," she confessed. "When I think about it, I feel like everyone had a pack"

"That's what I remember," said Drake.

"Same here," said Gracie.

"Me too," I said, nodding along with them. "My memory tells me the four of us each had a pack, but then, seeing as there are only the three, my memory must be wrong." I nudged my glasses up my nose. "All of our memories must be."

"Uh, what?" Drake asked, his frown deepening. "Our memories are *wrong*?" He shook his head. "What are you talking about?"

"Exactly what I said. Our memories are wrong. And more than wrong...*fake*."

"Woah Fiona, hold on a second," Saren said, also looking unconvinced. "Don't you think it's more likely we simply lost a pack along the way? We did just complete the *Doring Descent*," she said, motioning to the long shaft they'd entered from. The Doring Descent was the first section of the longest vertical pit in the Mora system. Even a hundred feet below the surface where Doring let out, the greater shaft, what familiar spelunkers called the Mora Abyss, kept going. "Maybe one of the packs fell into the abyss."

"Does anyone remember that happening?" I asked. When no one responded, I nodded. "Exactly. Because if that had happened, we would. Those packs are heavy, and the abyss isn't so deep that we wouldn't have heard it hit the bottom. On the contrary, we couldn't have missed it. The same goes if we'd lost the pack earlier. If only because Doring would've been impossible without it. Four people can't do that rappel with three packs." I shook my head. "No, there's no way."

"Okay so what, then?" Saren asked, the slightest hint of irritation in her voice. "How did the four of us get down here with only three packs?"

"That's the thing," I said, voice dropping low. "I don't think the four of us did."

"Fiona, what are you talking—?" Saren began spiritedly, her patience seeming to have all but run out. But then, quick as a headlamp shutting off, she stopped. Realization seemed to dawn on her face, and in an instant, all her fury fled for fear. "Hold on...you don't mean...?"

"Yes," I answered, looking at each group member in turn. "I think one of us isn't who they say they are. I think one of us is a *pretender*."

"A pretender?" Drake repeated. "What in the blazes is that?"

"I've only ever heard stories of them," I explained. "Arcane creatures that dwell in the dark...in forests and capes and caverns like this. They infiltrate groups and manipulate memories. Pose as companions, friends, even family. They make you think you know them, that you've known them for years, even, and that they've been there all along. But they haven't. They just got there. They tricked you. And now they're just pretending."

"Hold on, hold on, hold on, wait," Drake said, chopping the air with palms outstretched. "For years, you said? They trick you? How is that even possible?" He turned to Gracie and Saren for support. "I mean, it's not...right?"

Saren only shook her head. "Nothing's impossible. Not in this world. Not when it comes to the arcane."

A moment passed in silence. And it was a grave silence. Us being so far below the surface and insulated from its sounds, I swear I could hear my own blood stirring.

"Okay, so then what's the end game?" Drake asked finally, less skeptical than before, though still frowning hard. "This thing infiltrates our group, acts like it belongs, then what?"

"That's the thing," I said, still staring at the packs. "There is no endgame. Once a pretender infiltrates a group, it just stays there. It just keeps pretending."

Despite them being my own words, they made me shudder. Drake was still shaking his head.

"But I don't get it. Why? Why keep pretending? What's the point?"

"No one truly knows," I admitted with a shrug. "Some say it's how they eat, others believe they derive pleasure from it. Either way it's their nature. They'll do it their entire lives, and they'd do it for years on end if they could. Unfortunately, their magic can be...unsustainable."

"Unsustainable? What does that mean?"

"It means they kill us," Saren answered bluntly, and when Drake turned back to me in disbelief, I could only nod gravely.

"Having your memories rewritten like that, living a lie, it's not good for your brain. It scrambles it. Puts pressure in places there shouldn't be. Add enough, and you start to crack. Add more, that's when you break."

"Grave mercy," Drake muttered. "You mean to say they cause madness?"

"Given enough time, yes."

"Well how long is too long?" Drake demanded, eyes suddenly frantic. "Days? Years? If I had my memories to trust, I'd say I've known the lot of you for both of those and then some!"

"But that's not the truth," I reminded him.

"Well what is then?" He rounded on me. "How long has this imposter been among us?"

I shook my head. "There's no way to know for certain. However, given our unique circumstances—the secludedness of our location and the odd number of packs present—I believe that the pretender, whoever they are, just arrived."

"Let's see about these packs, then," Drake said, crossing to the pile of them. "Surely they're the key to this conundrum." He raised the first by its back strap. "Whose is this?"

"Mine," Saren, Gracie, and I said in unison, and I felt my heart sink.

"What?" Drake cried incredulously. He began to rifle through the bag's contents. "I thought this was mine!" He dropped the pack and practically pounced onto the next, ripping it open and dumping its contents onto the floor of the chamber. "Whose things are these?"

When no one responded, he did the same with the other. "Come on!" he cried. "Surely there must be some kind of identifier!"

But there wasn't. Not for me, anyway; the contents of each bag looked both as foreign and familiar as the last. And when no one else said different, I knew that the feeling must have been mutual.

"It's no use," I said finally, shaking my head at the ground. "Our memories are not our own. Our recollections can't be trusted."

"Blast it!" Drake cried, kicking one of the now empty packs. "How does this happen? How does it make any sense at all? If this creature is truly capable of such deceptions, why does it give itself away?" He gestured to the empty packs. "Why drop these breadcrumbs? Why not mask the inconsistencies? Why not leave us totally unaware?"

"Perhaps it likes it..." Gracie suggested quietly. "The taste of our paranoia."

"And is it not paranoid?" Drake asked. "That we should be aware of its presence?"

"The only way to know that would be to bring it to light."

"But how can we?" Saren asked, taking a step forward. Her wide eyes bored deeply into mine. "How can we whilst we're under its spell?"

"By using our wits," I said, meeting her stare with one of equal intensity. "We must not overestimate this threat. Its illusions are convincing, though not infallible." I gestured once more to the now empty packs. "Already it has erred. Whether intentionally or not, it matters little. This pretender has given us a clue. An opportunity. All's we need to do now is capitalize on it."

"I ask again, how?" Saren chimed, her expression unchanged. She looked around nervously. "Cut everyone's finger and see who bleeds black?"

I shook my head. "The pretender's disguise is better than that."

"Oh, but we can make him flinch, can't we?" Drake asked, clenching his fist. There was a dangerous glint in his eye. "Perhaps we bleed him out a little, see if then he doesn't show his true colors."

"Oh sure," I said with sarcasm. "And would you volunteer to be the first one bled?"

"Gladly," he said, and in a moment had his dive knife unsheathed. I felt myself recoil slightly.

"Grave shadows...are you mad? It was a jest, Drake. Slicing ourselves to bits isn't going to get us anywhere."

"A good way to see who's bluffing."

"Or a good way to get us all killed." I shook my head. "No, torment and intimidation won't work. The pretender won't betray itself until it's been either figured out or killed."

"So it can be killed, then?"

"It can. Or one of us instead. Would you volunteer to be first in that venture too?"

When he failed to immediately reply, I dared to hope that I'd finally gotten through to his better senses. Couldn't he see? This was a situation to be solved with reason, not physicality. That he held his knife aloft at all made me uneasy. Luckily, he soon sheathed it, and at the sight of its going, I think everyone breathed a sigh of relief.

"Okay, well what if we returned to the surface?" he asked next. "We could send word ahead of us to the village guard, inform them of our situation, and have them place a man with a telescope at the south tower. If they could see us coming—viewed from afar and through a lens no less—perhaps then they'd be able to identify the imposter. Perhaps then its magic would be out of range!"

"The pretender's magic is never out of range," I said grimly. "We take it back with us, we risk enslaving the entire village to its narrative."

"Shadows..." Drake muttered. "Are its powers truly so vast?"

I nodded. "A pretender is like a drop of poison. Only deadly if potent enough, though never good. A community might survive having one in its midst, though not unscathed. And the smaller the population, the greater the risk."

"Which is exactly why we can't go back," Saren agreed. She moved from one side of the cavern to the other, positioning herself across from Drake and the emptied packs. "And definitely why we can't send word of our situation. Were the village to know a pretender was among us, I doubt it'd be a telescope lens looking at us from the guard tower."

When the implication of what she'd said sunk in, Gracie's eyes went wide. "The village wouldn't do that," she squeaked. "W-would they?"

"If it's between us and them?" Saren said, then shook her head. "I don't see why not."

When Gracie turned her frightened eyes to me, I could only frown. I wasn't sure that Saren was correct in her assumption, but then, I wasn't sure that she was wrong either.

"Well we can at least go up to the surface, can't we?" Drake asked. "Return our eyes to the daylight? Down here in the darkness"—he fumbled some with his headlamp—"why...I can hardly see you at all."

Again I shook my head. Then laughed as I realized an entirely new element of our predicament. "There are only three packs." I looked from them and their scattered contents to the tunnel which led back up Doring. "We couldn't return to the surface even if we wanted to. Not without leaving someone behind, anyway. And then, even if we did leave one, it's a day's hike to the nearest town and we've only the provisions for three people and...Saren? Saren, what are you—? *Saren, stop!*"

She'd lunged forward suddenly, had pulled her knife from her belt and in an instant moved it to Drake's neck. Now it sat dangerously close to the flesh at his throat, a single motion from slitting him wide open.

"S-S-Saren," Drake managed, eyes wide, chin forced ever so slightly upward, body tensed as he was forced to keep perilously still. "Saren...what in blazes?"

When Saren only pressed her blade further, making Drake squirm, I took a step forward, shouted: "Saren, what are you doing?"

"Getting rid of our pretender," she replied, eyes never moving from Drake's frozen form. "Is it not obvious to you?" she asked. "All his questions. All his not knowing. Can't you see it for the charade it is? He's playing the fool, but it's not fooling me."

"Saren, wait...you're—you're wrong," Drake stammered, still not daring to move. In the murky light of our headlamps, I saw beads of sweat on his brow. "I'm not playing the fool. I—I *am* the fool! Think of our last three dives! I've been asking questions all along. You know how new I am to this."

"New to caving, or new to us?" Saren countered, and there was venom in her voice. "New to our minds?"

"Saren—" I began, taking another step forward, though stopped as Drake cried out.

The tip of Saren's knife had pricked him, had let a thin line of blood trickle down his neck. "You move another inch," she warned me, "and I push all the way through."

Now frozen myself, I hesitated even to speak. A moment passed in tight, agonizing tension. "Saren," I pleaded again, not moving. "Saren, *please*—"

"Saren, stop that right now!"

It was Gracie who shrieked, and her tone and volume were so much removed from that of their natural condition that even Saren seemed taken aback. In an instant of wide-eyed lucidity, she looked from Gracie, to Drake, and to the knife she held at his neck. Then, as if suddenly realizing herself, lowered the blade abruptly and stepped away.

"I...I'm sorry," she said, backing off from Drake in half-steps. She shook her head. "It's just that—"

"Saren," I interjected, "put the knife away."

She looked down and seemed startled to find it still in her hand, though she sheathed it immediately and took yet another step back. "I'm so sorry."

"Drake, are you okay?" I asked.

"Yeah," he said, rubbing at his neck with a palm. He shot Saren a look and her gaze fell.

"This won't be solved with violence," I said finally. "The pretender is smart. If we want to beat it, we'll need to be smarter."

Beside me, Gracie was nodding. "How do we do it?"

"Simple," I said, nudging my glasses up my nose. "We talk."

And so we did. We talked about our memories, our experiences, our childhoods and our origins. We left nothing out, went through each and every one of our relationships with precision, making sure all the details lined up. And they did, much to our dismay. So seamless was our collaborative narrative that after an hour of discussion, it actually seemed *less* likely that one of us could be an imposter, but that was just the nature of it. That was what made the pretender so good, and so dangerous.

Something needed to change. At the rate we were going, we would never figure it out. And the more we talked, the more we reaffirmed our altered memories, the more the notion of condemning any one of us became unthinkable. We were running out of time. Talking wasn't working. We needed another way.

And suddenly it hit me. A way that I alone could root out the imposter. The instant it came to me, I immediately diverted my mental focus, endeavoring, as well as I might, to conceal the idea in my subconscious. I did not know the full extent of our deceiver's mental powers, and I hesitated to conspire deliberately lest the potency of my own thoughts betray me. Though conspire I did, cautiously, taking care to devise my plan as absentmindedly as possible, fitting the pieces together only on the edges of my attention.

This idea, this scheme, it would need to be executed perfectly if there was any hope for it to work. And even then, I was not fully convinced that it would. There was a chance that the pretender had already accounted for it. Or perhaps was doing so right now, altering its spell just as quickly as I could think. If that was so, I needed to act fast. Even if this plan were doomed to fail, it seemed our only chance.

I let the conversation of the other three drown out before me, allowing my silent machinations to come center stage in my head. It was a risky thing to uncover them so, though a necessary one if I hoped to succeed. My timing needed to be perfect. My tone and delivery likewise. If I could get this right, I thought I could maybe throw the pretender off its instincts. Could maybe make it betray its instincts altogether. Only time would tell. I waited for my moment, and soon enough, it came.

"How about you, Fiona?" Drake asked. "Do you have any strange talents?"

I furrowed my brow as if to ponder, looking down though keeping myself well-aware of the three in company. I would need to watch their reactions. "Well, I can fold my tongue," I said, demonstrating. "There's the magic, of course." I snapped a finger, made a tiny flame appear at the tip of my finger. "And oh, I can wiggle my ears too." I presented this final talent and then watched carefully. Two reactions were already playing out.

"Fiona!" Drake cried, eyes wide. "You can...you're a—?"

"Arcane," Saren finished, equally awestruck. She and Drake had reacted much as I'd expected, both of them having jolted as if struck by a lightning bolt. The only one who hadn't jumped, the only one who'd failed to react to my little trick, was Gracie.

She was good, though.

In an instant, her eyes were as wide as the others. Had I not been watching so closely, I might have missed the difference, might have taken them to be genuine. But they weren't. There'd been a delay there, a fraction of a second in which she'd had no reaction at all, and then, sensing the response of the others, had shifted to follow suit. Had mimicked them, and in a moment blended in near perfectly.

Near.

"Are you not surprised, Gracie?" I asked, turning on her.

She smiled at me. "I'm sorry?"

"My arcana," I said, snapping my finger and making the flame appear once more. "Does the sight of it not startle you?"

"Why, of course! It's...it's amazing!" she said with a flourish, and though still she smiled, I thought I detected a wariness about her. Like a dog with its hackles up. I needed to tread carefully.

"Are you sure? Compared to Drake and Saren"—I gestured to the two of them—"why, it's like you already knew."

"Well you *did* already tell me." Gracie laughed, staring at me intently. "Don't you remember?"

And suddenly I did. Suddenly it was there, vivid as any other—the memory of telling Gracie, alone, my one big secret. It was a vivid memory. A strong one. Though another was stronger.

Got you.

"No I didn't," I said, and I took a step forward. "I've never told anyone."

And I knew that to be true. So true...so fundamental to my being...that even the false memory could not sully it. I could not have made an exception for Gracie, not without making exceptions for Saren and Drake too. For my mother and father. For Mateo. No, it did not align. As strong as the memory may have seemed, the way it contradicted everything else assured me of its falsehood.

I took another step, and this time Drake and Saren stepped with me, the three of us closing in on Gracie. Sizing her up anew, trying to see her for what she truly was.

"Fiona, please...you've got this wrong," she pleaded. "I swear I am who I say! Please...please you must believe me!"

She put up a good show—those big, brown eyes of hers filling with what appeared to be genuine fear and dismay as the three of us, her so-called friends, backed her further and further into a corner of the chamber. She continued to beg and plead, even got on her knees and weeped once she could retreat no longer, though it was all for nought. We'd figured her out, and eventually, she—or rather, *it*—seemed to accept it.

"What a pity," she said, and at first did not move from her prostrate position. Though her voice had changed. With a start, I realized that a single eye peered up at me despite her head facing down. "And I was having so much fun."

She grinned then, and it was a grin entirely not her own. But then, perhaps it was. For she had never been her, and my perception of what was hers, never anything. As she began to rise, uncoiling herself like a snake, she seemed to change. The way she stood, her posture, the very shape of her. She fell into the shadows before the transformation was complete, whispering, in a voice that seemed both childlike and knowing, "Goodbye."

Saren made a lunge for the thing, but it was quick, and within seconds it was gone. In the dim beams of our darting headlamps, I managed to catch a glimpse of it as it went, a dark, slithering mass contorting itself into a crevice much too small for a person, or even a light, to follow. Back into the depths it went. Back into those small places only it could inhabit. Waiting for another group of spelunkers to forget its headcount, and then remember one more. Waiting for another opportunity to prey. Waiting, in that everlasting darkness, to pretend.

About the Author

Kieran Wiesenberg is an indie author from western New York. Find out more at kieranwiesenberg.com

ALSO BY KIERAN WIESENBERG

The Wolf of Wilmore Manor
Fearnomena
The Arcane Amnesiac

www.ingramcontent.com/pod-product-compliance
Lightning Source LLC
Chambersburg PA
CBHW021935170626
46807CB00007B/3123